It's a Squirrely Life

JP Cawood

ISBN: 978-0-9983786-8-8

i

TABLE OF CONTENTS

ACKNOWLEDGMENTS

Story by JP Cawood and Michael Cawood
Cover Illustration by Denny Minonne
Published by HEROmation

CHAPTER ONE

"Freeze! This is a bank robbery!"

George, a young squirrel wearing a sporty hoodie, puts his hands up with fear in his eyes.

"Please don't hurt me!" George pleads with the robbers. Two younger squirrels with ski-masks over their faces point sticks at George.

One robber hands him a burlap sack and says, "Gimme all your nuts." George takes the sack and stuffs it full.

A young female squirrel, Mary, hugs a baby squirrel to her chest. Unlike George, she's fearless, and looks directly at the robbers.

"You won't get away with this. Bad guys never win," she says.

"Please, Mary. Don't make them mad," says George as he hands the sack to the robbers. They take the stash and run away, laughing.

Mary says to George, "You can't let them get away with this."

"No one needs to lose a life today," George says. Mary rolls her eyes and hands him the baby.

"If you won't stop them, I will." Mary chases the robbers. They look back and see her coming.

"Run!" The robbers pick up their pace. One of them slams into a Christmas tree and falls. Mary tackles him and rips off his ski mask.

"Hey, I know you!" she says.

The other robber looks back and trips over a toy on the floor. Mary grabs the sack from him as he pulls off his mask.

"No fair, Mary," whines the robber. "Of course you're faster than us. You're our big sister!"

Mary laughs and says, "I told you. Bad guys never win." She empties the sack. Wooden blocks fall out onto the floor. It was all pretend. They are not in a bank. They're in the living room of a small tree house. The bank robbers are George and Mary's younger brothers, Chester and Lester.

"Okay, I'm the banker now!" Chester squeals. "George, you be the bad guy this time."

George scratches his head and says, "Um, I'm not sure I'd be good at that."

Their grandmother, Greta, appears behind George with the help of a walker.

"I'm not sure how good you are at a lot of things," Greta says to George. He turns around to find her right behind him.

"Ah!" he shrieks, surprised that she's so close.

Mary sticks up for George. "Leave him alone, Grannie. We were just having a little fun."

"George, you're late. You know I need your help at the bank again today," Greta says. She bites into an apple loudly, leaving only the core. She tosses it on the floor and asks George to pick it up for her.

George hands the baby squirrel to Mary, who sighs and passes the baby to Greta.

"I'd love to play more," George says to Chester and Lester, "but I have to go to work to protect the real bank. Let the countdown to Christmas begin!"

"We'll be ready in time," Mary says. "Can I help at the bank, Grannie?"

"George will help me," Greta says to Mary. "You can watch your brothers."

Mary tries to explain that she wants to help at the bank, but George says, "Thanks, sis. I've got it covered."

"You can't run a bank dressed like that," Greta says. "Where's that cute tie I bought you?"

George groans. "I don't think the customers mind a more casual vibe."

Grannie yells at George to put the tie on. He quickly takes off his hoodie and put on a velvet jacket and tie.

His grannie smiles. "That's better. Now kiss your family goodbye. I'll catch up with you later."

George cringes as he gives Greta a kiss. He fist-bumps Chester and Lester and then kisses the baby.

The baby spits up on his jacket. He moans while Mary, Greta, Chester, and Lester laugh. George quickly changes into another jacket and leaves for work.

"Wait, George. Don't forget this." Greta hands George a ledger book with all the bank's transactions. She tells him to be very careful with it. He promises to protect it.

***

George walks out into the busy city of Oak Creek. Animals hustle through the trees; squirrels, birds, ants, chipmunks, rabbits, and mice. Two squirrels coming from different directions crash into each other, causing a line of squirrels waiting to climb down the tree.

George moans. "Looks like a 30 squirrel pile up. I think I'll take the track."

Moments later, George joins a group of animals on a subway-like platform. A badger pulls the long plank through the tree trunk, down into an underground tunnel.

A rat next to George whips his tail around as he holds a pair of seashells up to his ears like headphones. His tail hits George in the face. George patiently moves it aside, but it whips him again. He politely endures the non-stop whipping to the beat of the rat's music.

The platform bursts out of the ground and onto grass. It stops, and George jumps off. New animals jump on.

George steps out onto Main Street. He passes an Oak Creek sign that marks the town center. Tall trees protect the open square. A Christmas tree stands in the middle. Mice decorate the tree with berries, ants carry garland, and birds hang mistletoe. The animals are getting ready for Christmas.

Shops line the town center in the bases of the surrounding trees. Squirrels sell goods from stalls and sit in cafes. At the gym, animals run on treadmills made of wood and rocks, with nuts hanging over their heads to motivate them. A flock of butterflies fly overhead.

A rabbit with a fake leg carries groceries. He struggles to open the door of a shop. George runs over to hold the door open for him.

"Thanks George!"

"My pleasure!" says George as he continues on. He waves hello to a few animals he passes. An old squirrel walking in front of him drops a seed. George picks it up.

"Excuse me, Stewart. You dropped your seed."

"What's that, George?" the old squirrel asks. "I peed? Aw, not again!" The deaf old squirrel checks his pants for a wet spot.

George repeats himself loudly. "Your seed. You dropped your seed."

"Stampede? Where?!" Old Squirrel Stewart looks around, scared. "Now I really need to pee," he adds.

George hands the seed back to him and walks away.

"Ah, a banker without greed!" Stewart says to himself.

George takes an elevator up a large tree and gets off on the 5th floor, home to the Oak Creek Bank. He unlocks the front door with his key and steps inside.

George opens the teller window and organizes nuts and seeds into a wooden cash register. Then he opens the vault to find piles of nuts, seeds, sticks, and berries.

Markings on the wall shows the vault is 4/5ths full. George pulls out the ledger book with all the bank's transactions. He reviews it and mumbles to himself, "You can, and will, fill this vault before the first big storm. Cutting it close this year... Christmas is coming."

A customer calls from the teller station, "Good morning, Greta!"

George closes the vault and walks to the teller station where Maddy, the well-dressed Queen of the ant colony, stands waiting for him.

"Maddy! Just the ant I wanted to see. Ready to deposit the colony's weekly stash?"

"Where's your grandmother?" Maddy asks.

"She's running a little late, but will be here soon. I can help with your deposit."

"Okay, darling." Maddy snaps her fingers, and soldier ants bring their stash in like an assembly line.

5

Noel, a flying squirrel with cape-like wings, glides through the door with her younger brother, Junior, as the ants toil.

George greets her. "Good morning, Noel. Making a deposit today?"

Noel whispers, "Withdraw I'm afraid. Junior lost his first tooth and we'll be leaving it for the Squirrel Fairy." Noel's brother, Junior, gives George a grin, showing off his missing tooth.

"How exciting!" George says loudly. Then he whispers to Noel, "But your account has a negative balance already."

Maddy eavesdrops as the ants bring in her large deposit.

Noel whispers back. "This foraging season has been so dangerous. Lots of bear sightings, as you know. My family has really been struggling."

George whispers to Noel, "What's one more seed going to hurt? You'll pay it back soon enough. We're in this together, friend."

He takes a seed out and hands it to Noel. Maddy watches with a raised antenna.

"You're the best, George!" Noel exclaims.

"Losing a front tooth is a huge deal. Congratulations, Junior," says George.

Junior smiles, showing off his missing tooth again. Noel and Junior leave the bank happy. George makes a note of the lost seed in the ledger. A big burly squirrel enters next.

"Hey. How'd the foraging go last night, Burly?" George asks.

Big Burly drops a few nuts, seeds, and berries onto the table. "I had to make a run for my life!"

"Not again…" George says with a gasp.

"That's right. The bear!" exclaims Burly. "Its growls were louder than the waterfall."

Maddy gasps. George remembers that she's there, listening.

"I've got a family of twenty at home. I can't be a hero," says Big Burly.

George nods. "Right. Don't worry, we're in this together." George puts on a brave face as Big Burly leaves. He marks Burly's small deposit in the ledger and turns to Maddy.

"All set with your deposit, Maddy?"

She shakes her head. "I'm afraid we won't be making a deposit today after all, George."

George can't believe his ears. "But…"

"I have thousands of ants to consider," says Maddy. "If the bank is struggling, we must reconsider our options. I'm sure your grandmother will understand." Maddy snaps her fingers twice. The assembly line reverses.

A clumsy ant, Tony, doesn't hear the command and passes his nut forward while the next ant passes one back. Tony juggles two nuts as more come crashing down onto his head. Maddy rolls her eyes at Tony's mistake.

George catches four nuts before they fall on Tony, two in his paws and two with his feet. He supports himself with his tail, balancing the nuts as he speaks with Maddy.

"There's still another week before Christmas. We always have enough nuts saved by then. My grannie will be here soon to explain everything to you." George tosses the nuts back to Tony.

Tony juggles the nuts well at first, but soon loses control, sending them toppling onto his head.

"I know when Christmas is," says Maddy. "I can't have my workers breaking their backs for the benefit of other animals. I'm afraid we must pull our entire inventory."

George begs Maddy not to take all her nuts from the bank. He promises Greta will be there soon. He hopes that is true, but lately Grannie hasn't been coming to the bank at all because of her bad back.

Maddy smiles with pity. "Please know it is with a heavy heart that we must take our business elsewhere. I'll send some of my workers over to collect the rest of our stash later. Do take care, George. Send your grandmother my regards."

Maddy walks out with her head held high. George feels sad and doesn't know what to do.

Tony the ant scrambles to pick up as many nuts as he can carry. He asks another ant, "What's going on? What are we doing?" He drops another nut and bumps into ants as the assembly line reverses out of the bank.

"We're taking everything… back?" Tony moans. "But it was so much work getting it here."

The other ants do not respond and stick to the task at hand. They pick up their nuts and march toward the door. Tony picks up the nut he dropped. His back cracks under the weight of it.

"The Queen knows best!" Tony says with a strained smile.

George looks at his ledger with sadness. "Oh, dear. How will we have enough nuts saved before Christmas now?"

CHAPTER TWO

Later that evening, George closes the door to the bank as his silly squirrel friend, Ángel, hops over.

"Hey, amigo! How's your tail hanging?" Ángel asks.

George doesn't answer.

"What's up with the tie, amigo?"

George shrugs.

Ángel asks George what's wrong, but he doesn't answer. He pulls out his keys to lock the bank door.

Ángel tries to cheer George up. "Let's go hang with the homies. They're at Nick's. That'll make you feel better."

George shakes his head. "I have to get home. Grannie didn't come into the bank today, and I have something important to tell her."

Ángel grabs George and shakes him. "I swore an oath to the forest gods to never let a friend go home sad."

"What? Why?" George asks.

"You could wind up in the nuthouse." Ángel laughs.

George rolls his eyes and moves toward the door to lock it.

Ángel steals his keys. "Yoink!"

"Hey, Ángel, give 'em back!"

Ángel throws the keys and then races to catch them, playing keep away with himself. He's fast! George is too tired to play along. Ángel catches the keys again and leaps into a victory dance.

"Fine, I'll go to Nick's, but only or a few minutes," George says.

Ángel smiles. "You won't regret it, amigo." He throws the keys back to George and walks him toward the tree elevator.

George leaves without locking the door to the bank. It creaks open a crack. Maddy steps out of the shadows with an evil look in her eyes. A small army of ants stands behind her.

"Okay troops, get in there and take what's ours," Maddy says.

Tony steps forward and points to a sign that says closed. "Shouldn't we come back tomorrow? The bank is closed."

Maddy says, "Ants wait for no one!" She pushes the unlocked door open.

"Of course, my Queen," says Tony as the ants file inside.

***

George and Ángel walk on a tree branch toward their friend Nick's hole in the tree.

"You're working way too hard," Ángel says to George. "You deserve to have fun like the rest of us kids."

Noel the flying squirrel jumps from branch to branch, gliding on her wings with Christmas garland in one paw.

Ángel stops and stares at her as she glides gracefully and hangs her garland on the tree. She backflips and nails the landing. Noel waves hello to George and Ángel.

Ángel leans toward the tree to act cool, but misses and face plants onto the ground.

Noel's garland falls off the tree. Ángel scrambles to catch it.

"Can I help, Noel?" he asks.

"Sure. Thanks, Ángel."

Ángel grabs the garland and tries to hang it on the branch above. George and Noel watch him fail miserably. He doesn't have super cool wings like Noel does.

Chase, a bird with a red racing stripe down his back, flies over.

"What are you doing, Ángel?" Chase asks. "This isn't a job for a basic squirrel."

"I'm nut basic. I'm Ángel!"

Chase rolls his eyes. "I don't have time for the flying impaired."

Ángel puffs out his chest and climbs the tree with garland in hand. He jumps with arms outstretched, but instead of gliding, he bellyflops at George's feet.

"You call that flying?" Chase laughs and picks up the garland. He soars over a branch and then flies circles around Ángel, causing the squirrel to spin out and fall.

Chase laughs and says, "Gotta jet. See you later, George. Try to keep up, Noel."

"Gotta fly," Noel says to George and Ángel. "I'm helping Chase decorate in exchange for babysitting my brother."

Chase sticks his head back in from out of nowhere. "For the record, I am not a babysitter. Junior looks up to me, so I hang with the little guy. Okay?" Chase zips away as fast as he came. Noel follows him, gliding away on her super cool wing flaps.

Ángel watches her go. He tells George that he wishes he could be a flying squirrel. It looks like so much fun!

George puts his arm around Ángel's shoulder and walks him to Nick's hole in the tree.

"Come on, I don't have much time to hang," George reminds his friend.

***

Back at the bank, the line of ants passes nuts, seeds, berries, and sticks out the door. Maddy supervises with a smug smile.

"Ma'am, how much of the stash is ours?" Tony asks.

Maddy laughs and says, "All of it!"

"Yes, my Queen." Tony picks up a large nut, and his back cracks. He hides his pain as he passes the nut and picks up another one.

***

George and Ángel walk into Nick's hole. The place is covered in spider webs, but there's also a pool table and a basket of wooden toys. George's feet stick to the floor.

"Someone forgot to take down their Halloween decorations," George says.

"Who?" asks Nick. He's a giant spider!

George pulls at his stuck foot and stumbles backward. Ángel sits next to a Woodpecker with wild eyes.

"Another, Nick," the Woodpecker says.

Nick slides a piece of wood in front of the Woodpecker, who licks his beak and pecks the wood to bits in seconds. He sighs with relief.

George pulls webbing from his foot and sits next to Ángel, who asks the Woodpecker, "Rough day, amigo?"

"I'm stressing!" says Woodpecker. "All this talk about that bear really has me shook."

"How bad could he be?" asks George.

"The bear is a hundred feet tall with fangs that can break rock. He's so hungry, he'd eat another bear! But mostly, he settles for nuts, seeds, wood, and squirrels. Juicy, juicy squirrels."

George groans and says, "Got any almond milk, Nick? I need some liquid courage."

"Want some venom?" asks Nick the Spider. "That'll really give you a kick in the nuts."

"Does it do anything for stress?" George asks.

"No, but it'll grow legs on your chest," Nick says.

George declines Nick's venom.

Ángel says, "Sounds like this bear could ruin Christmas."

"We need the bear gone or we're all doomed! Doomed, I tell ya!" says Woodpecker. He goes in on another piece of wood.

George checks his ledger. He holds it close to his chest and says to himself, "Yes… Doomed! I don't know what to do if we don't fill the bank vault by Christmas."

"That's your grannie's problem, not yours," Nick says. George says nothing. No one knows that he's been running the bank by himself for a while now.

Ángel walks to a pool table and grabs a stick. He hits the "balls" which are actually curled up beetles. "I really wish I was a flying squirrel," he says. "How cool would that be?"

George grabs a stick and joins Ángel in the game. He

takes a turn hitting the beetle balls, but misses his shot.

Ángel hits a beetle with his stick, and it rolls around the table. The beetle uncurls and waddles into the corner pocket, scoring a point for Ángel. George does a double take.

"I think my eyes are playing tricks on me," George says. "I have been working at the bank a lot lately."

"Tell your grannie to stop working you so hard," Nick says. If only it were that simple.

"I can't say that to my grannie. She's one tough squirrel."

Woodpecker chimes in. "If the bear doesn't get dealt with, no one will have a family to complain about!"

George thinks. It will be hard to tell Greta that the ants are pulling their part of the stash. The more he thinks about it, the more it scares him to tell her. He walks to the door without saying anything.

"Hey, where are you going?" Ángel asks.

"I've got something to do," George says as he leaves.

"Sounds mysterious. Cashew later amigo!" Ángel turns to Woodpecker and says, "You got him all riled up. Tu eres un chismoso."

"I'm not a gossip. I tell it like it is!" Woodpecker demolishes more wood.

Ángel miraculously sinks the rest of the beetles into the pockets in a surprise trick shot.

***

George heads into the forest to forage for nuts. It's dark outside at night. He rubs his tired eyes as he walks through the woods. He checks his ledger and looks back toward town. George closes the book, nods, and proceeds.

He thinks if he can find enough nuts, maybe he won't have to tell Greta about the ant problem.

George sniffs the ground and digs. He pulls up a moldy apple core. He recoils and looks up to see his Grannie standing in front of him.

"Ah!" He rubs his eyes and doesn't see Greta. His tired mind must be playing tricks on him.

George sighs and continues on. He climbs a tree, loses his grip, and slides down to the ground, leaving claw marks in the bark.

"I didn't ask to take over the bank. I'm too young for this much work," George says to himself as he scales the tree and sniffs his way down a branch. He loses his balance and falls. He catches the branch and holds on for dear life, struggling to pull himself back up.

"Just wait until they see how much I forage. Grannie never needs to know that Maddy wants all her nuts back."

He falls to the ground and lands in a bush. The leaves shake. He runs out covered in ticks, so he frantically drops and rolls.

"I have nothing to prove! Especially not to my silly old grannie. Maybe I will tell her the truth about the ants."

In the distance, George hears a roar that startles him.

"The bear!"

CHAPTER THREE

As the sun rises, George stumbles into the town center with a few seeds in his arms. Not a great forage, but it's something. He climbs up into his tree house.

He tiptoes into his bedroom, takes off his jacket and tie, and lies down. Just as George closes his eyes, his baby cries. He moans and sits up, ready to start again.

George joins his family in the kitchen. Mary fries almonds on a fire stove while she holds the baby. George falls asleep at the table as Chester and Lester run around the room.

Greta enters with her walker. She sits down at the table and eats apples at rapid speed; they go in her mouth whole and come out cored. She throws the cores in a pile on the floor and tells George to pick them up for her when she's done. He's asleep and doesn't hear her.

"George, are you listening?" Greta throws an apple core to wake him up.

"Huh?!" George wakes up.

Mary hands the baby to Greta. "You okay, bro? If you're too tired to help Grannie at the bank today, I can do it."

Greta says, "George can handle it." She passes the baby to George. The baby spits up on him. He sighs.

"Grannie, I have something important to tell you."

"What is it, George?"

He's scared Grannie will be mad about Maddie taking her stash back, so he says nothing.

"Go on, speak up," Grannie says.

George hopes Maddy will change her mind. In fact, he will go see her after breakfast to make sure the ants to stay with Oak Creek Bank.

"Will you make it into the bank today?" George asks.

"I'll try," Greta says.

"If you need help," Mary adds.

"George can handle it," Greta says. "Don't forget to wear your tie, George."

He nods.

"Where is the ledger?" Greta asks. "I forgot to get it from you yesterday."

"I have it, Grannie. Everything is under control," George says.

****

After breakfast, George leaves home with tired eyes. He runs into a big pileup on the tree route caused by Old Squirrel Stewart.

A chipmunk with a high-pitch voice yells, "Hey old man, get off the tree!"

"Did I pee?" asks Stewart. "Not again…"

George takes the subway instead. He falls asleep standing as the platform makes its way downtown. The same music-loving rat whips George in the face. George wakes up, but then falls right back to sleep. Wake, sleep, wake, sleep, repeat to the beat of the rat's music.

George walks to the front door of the Oak Creek Bank like a zombie, with keys in hand. The front door is already open a crack. That jolts him awake, and he enters.

Inside, he finds the vault is open and empty. The bank has been ransacked! Standing in the center of the chaos is the ant queen, Maddy. She turns around.

"Oh, George! What's happened?" Maddy asks.

"I... I don't know."

"I found the bank like this," Maddy lies. "Who could have broken into a locked bank?"

George looks at the keys in his hand. His eyes grow the size of saucers as he realizes what's happened. He forgot to lock the door last night!

Maddy says, "It must have been that bear! Sound the alarm. We must tell the town!"

Oh no, George is in big trouble now! "Wait, let me think," he says.

"George, I know you're worried about paying us back what you owe, but we can deal with that later. For now, we must warn the others."

George is speechless. Maddy peels an apple core off the back of George's jacket.

"How uncivilized, George." Maddy throws the core as she exits.

George follows, still trying to process what's happened.

Maddy walks out of the bank and leans over the tree branch. She yells down to her ants and snaps her fingers. From the town center below, Tony and the soldier ants look up at their queen. They link arms, forming a ladder up to her. Maddy walks onto Tony's head at the top of the ladder. He smiles up at her, despite her foot in his eye.

They carry her down gently into the town center. One more snap of her fingers, and the ants form a raised platform for Maddy to stand on.

"Attention Oak Creek! There has been a robbery!" Maddy yells.

The town's animals stop in their tracks and turn to Maddy.

Ángel asks, "Whoa, what happened?"

"There's a big bad bear on the prowl, and it's taken everything from the bank. Everything!" Maddy declares.

Everyone gasps at the news. Woodpecker goes crazy and bores his head into a tree. Tony, breaking his back to hold the ant formation, looks up, confused.

"Oh no! A bear broke into the bank?" Tony asks. "Wow! That's scary."

Panic moves through town. George makes his way to the center. Greta pops up out of nowhere in her walker, holding the baby.

"Ah!" George yells at Greta's surprise pop up.

"What did you do, George?" Greta asks.

George doesn't know what to say. He's ruined everything.

Greta hands the baby to George. She addresses the town. "Don't fear, I will sort this out. The guilty party will be found and punished. The stash will be recovered."

George sweats. It's his fault he forgot to lock the door.

Mary finds him in the crowd. "There you are, brother. Are you all right?"

Greta says, "First, I will…" Before she can finish her sentence, she faints from the stress of it all!

"Grannie!" Mary calls out. She and George go to Greta's side. "What are we going to do, George?"

Maddy turns to George and says, "Yes, George. What is

the bank going to do?"

The crowd turns their attention to George. He clutches the baby to his chest.

"Well, um…"

"How will we bring the guilty party to justice?" Maddy asks. All eyes are on George.

"I… I'm not sure."

Maddy keeps pressing. "How will we survive the winter?"

George stammers. "I… I don't know yet, but we're in this toget—

Maddy interrupts. "Have no fear Oak Creek! Luckily, we made the wise decision to keep the ant colony's stash separate this year. We will share. After all, we're in this together." She smiles slyly as the animals collectively sigh with relief. Maddy adds, "We will accept the deeds to your homes as collateral for each loan."

Shock and horror from the crowd.

"Maddy, that would mean you'd own all of Oak Creek," George says.

"Only if the loans aren't paid back. We'll be fair and give everyone until New Year."

Big Burly chimes in. "New Year? We can't forage in winter!"

The chipmunk with the high voice asks, "What are we going to do?"

Another chipmunk, with a surprisingly deep voice, adds, "Yeah!"

"The new Ant Creek Bank will open tomorrow, ready to service all of your holiday needs. Merry Christmas everyone!" Maddy jumps off her platform. The soldier ants reform as a security perimeter around her, moving Maddy through the crowd like a celebrity.

All the town's animals talk at once, trying to figure out what to do.

George follows the ants. "Maddy! Please, let's talk about this."

"Don't worry, George. We'll gladly accept your loan application tomorrow as well. Toodles!" Maddy's soldier ants whisk her away, leaving George in their dust.

George tries to hand the baby to Mary, but she refuses.

"Not yet," Mary says. One second later, the baby spits up on George's shoulder. Then Mary grabs the baby.

George sighs. Not only does he have vomit all over him, his grannie isn't feeling well. He feels guilty for forgetting to lock the door, and does not know how to save Christmas.

CHAPTER FOUR

George and Mary stand behind the teller station amongst the rubble of the ransacked bank.

"George, what are you going to do?" Mary asks. "How can I help?"

George licks his finger and lifts it to the air. "There's a storm brewing. I can feel it."

Noel flies into the bank. "Tails up! Everyone's on their way."

Angry animals quickly fill the bank. They hold up receipts with panic on their faces. Ángel pops in, too.

George addresses the crowd. "I'm glad you're here. I have some news for you, folks. We are a powerful community and if we work together, we can replenish before the first snow falls."

The chipmunk with the high voice says, "But, George, we've been struggling all season."

The chipmunk with the deep voice adds, "Yeah!"

"It could snow any minute!" says Big Burly.

"Yeah!" adds the chipmunk with the deep voice again.

The rabbit with the fake leg says, "And there's a bear on the loose!"

"Yeah!" adds the chipmunk with the deep voice again.

"You're thinking about this all wrong. We're in this together," George says.

Big Burly chimes in again. "That's what Maddy said, too."

The chipmunk with the high voice says, "I had ten nuts, twenty-one seeds, ten sticks, and a berry in this bank. And it's all gone."

George pulls out the ledger. "I know. It's all in here."

Several animals in the crowd ask where Greta is.

"She's resting," George says. "You're in good hands with me."

"But you're just a kid!" an animal shouts.

The chipmunk adds, "Maddy will loan us what we need for Christmas. We're better off at the ant bank!"

"Yeah!" adds the chipmunk with the deep voice again. A few customers move toward the door with chatter about going to the anthill.

George reminds them that if they can't pay her loan back by New Year, the ants will take over their tree houses. "If you stick with Oak Creek Bank, we'll...'

"Her loan will buy us time," says Big Burly.

Chase the bird reminds everyone, "There's not much time before the storms start."

"Come on, gang. We can do this. But we have to stick together," says George.

"We've got mouths to feed," says Big Burly. "I'm sorry, George. I have to go with Maddy on this one."

Customers leave one by one.

Rabbit walks up to George. "Here, you might need this." He takes off his fake foot and hands it to George.

"For good luck," Rabbit says.

"Thanks, but you can keep it."

Rabbit shrugs, pops his leg back on, and leaves.

Noel lingers. Chase tells her it's time to jet. She approaches George and says, "I'm sorry, George."

George nods solemnly as the last customers leave. Ángel and Mary are the only ones left.

Ángel says, "Hey, amigo."

George doesn't want to hear any of his friend's jokes. "Not now, Ángel."

"But we're in this together."

"I said not now."

"Okay, amigo. Cashew later." Ángel leaves with a sad, limp tail.

"We can't do this alone, George," Mary says. "Especially when Grannie needs to rest."

"Grannie hasn't been to the bank in a while. This is my job, and I won't give up."

"Maybe we should take a loan from Maddy too," Mary says.

George refuses. "If we borrow anything under her terms, we'd lose our home. And so will everyone else if they turn to her. I don't want to talk about it any more tonight, okay?"

Mary huffs out of the bank, leaving George all alone. He stays there all night, thinking. He knows he can't forage enough nuts by himself, but he also knows he can't take Maddy's loan. What should he do?

***

Later that night, he sneaks into his tree house to check on Greta. She's snoring loudly. He checks on Chester and

Lester. They're also asleep. He kisses them goodbye, then stops at the baby's wooden crib. He bends down to kiss the baby, who wakes up! The baby babbles.

"Shhhhhh! Don't wake Grannie." George picks up the baby, and it spits up all over him. He sighs. The baby rests its head on his shoulder and falls asleep. George hugs him tight before putting him back into his crib.

George tiptoes outside. He closes his front door quietly, turns around, and runs into Greta.

"Ah!"

"Where do you think you're going?" Greta asks.

"I have to fix this."

"Maybe I gave you too much work, too soon," she admits.

"I can handle it," he says. "Lay down and rest."

George pushes past her. She follows him with her walker, painfully slow.

"Whatever you do, don't lose the ledger!" she calls out as he leaves the tree house.

It's dark outside, and the town is quiet. George runs down Main Street. He hears voices up ahead, so he ducks for cover. He stumbles, trips, and falls. George dives behind the center Christmas tree just as the two chipmunks walk by. He overhears the chipmunk with the high voice say, "George really messed everything up big time."

The chipmunk with the deep voice says, "Yeah."

George peeks his head out as they walk away. He makes a run for it, but trips and falls again. He picks himself up and walks into the forest.

Noel and Chase talk in the woods. George hides in a bush and listens.

Chase says, "You could fly south with me for the winter."

"That's too far for me to travel. I would slow you down. Besides, you know my family needs me here to help watch Junior."

"I am super fast," Chase boasts, "but I could slow down a bit for you."

"I better get home. Can you babysit Junior for me tomorrow so I can try to help forage?"

"Yes, but… Don't. Tell. Anyone!" Chase says.

Noel smiles and they run off through the trees.

George feels bad that Chase is thinking about leaving for Christmas. He's one of the few birds that sticks around in winter, and Oak Creek wouldn't be the same without him. George steps out of the bush and walks through the trees.

Next, he stumbles upon Ángel as he jumps off a branch. He's practicing being a flying squirrel, but since he doesn't have the wing flaps, he falls on his face.

Nearby leaves rustle.

"Who's there?" Ángel asks. George steps out from behind a tree.

"Hey amigo. You okay?"

George huffs. "The bank is empty. The ants will own the town. Christmas is ruined. But I'm doing great. Thanks for asking." He jumps onto another tree and scurries up the trunk. Ángel follows.

"I know this is scary, but we'll be okay, George. Let's go back and work it out."

George says, "I can't go back." They jump from one tree to another.

"Why nut?" asks Ángel.

"It's all my fault. Everyone hates me."

"It's nut your fault the bear broke into the bank."

George stops at the edge of a branch. "But I left

the…"

The truth about the door being unlocked gets stuck in George's throat. He hasn't said it out load to anyone.

"I… I'm leaving town. I give up." George jumps to the next branch with Ángel right behind.

"You can't! We can figure something out. We can save Christmas!"

George scurries down a tree trunk and jumps back on the ground. "There's nothing we can do, Ángel. It's too late."

Ángel jumps off and falls into George, toppling him. "There must be some solution, amigo."

Just then, the first snow of the season begins to fall. George makes a note of it in his ledger.

"Oh no! How could we ever forage enough so quickly? We'd need an amazing plan."

"I know someone who can give us a little Christmas magic." Ángel marches through two bushes, and George follows. They walk for a while, and George follows Ángel toward a valley filled with beautiful butterflies.

"Where are we going, Ángel? We don't have time…"

"Shhhh. We're here."

As they approach, the butterflies fly up all around them, revealing the entrance to a kooky little hut made of cocoon shells. George is hesitant, but follows Ángel inside.

A furry caterpillar named CP sits on a chair made of green leaves. The wall behind him is full of beakers and vials with strange liquids inside.

CP greets Ángel. "Hey, buddy. It's been too long. I miss playing chess and musing on life together."

"Musing on life?" George asks. Ángel doesn't answer.

"What can I do for ya?" CP asks.

Ángel sits cross-legged around a fire in the middle of

the hut and says, "We've got a bear problem."

George sniffs a caldron that bubbles atop the fire. He's unable to relax.

"Time is of the essence," George adds, clutching the ledger to his chest. He paces and whispers to Ángel, "I don't see how a caterpillar can help us restock the bank." He then says to CP, "No offense."

"Bias is always offensive," says CP.

"That's true," Ángel adds.

George throws his head in his hands. "I'm a terrible squirrel!"

Ángel comforts George. "Come on, you're the best. You've just had a really nutty day."

"Looks like someone needs a swaddle," CP says as he dips an acorn cup into the steamy caldron and hands the drink to George.

George sniffs it. "Smells... oaky?"

"Hints of cinnamon with a bold after taste," says CP. "I've searched the forest for that perfect zest. The lemon trees that mark the path toward the waterfall were the missing ingredient to make the recipe really sing."

George takes a sip. He looks pleasantly surprised and drinks the rest of the glass in one gulp. "Thanks. I needed that."

"Let's start over," CP says. "What happened?"

George takes a deep breath. "I went back to the bank after a night of foraging and found it empty. Everything was... gone. It's my job to keep it stocked for winter."

"Isn't it your grannie's job?" Ángel asks.

"It's complicated," George replies. "Christmas is almost here, and I've let the entire town down... Oak Creek would be better off without me."

"How do you zest a lemon?" Ángel asks CP.

"Here, I'll show you."

"Can we stay focused?" George asks, annoyed.

Ángel says, "Dude, it's nut your fault."

George says, "You're right, amigo. It could be your fault! You took my keys away and distracted me. Now everything is ruined."

"I was just trying to help!" Ángel says.

George's eyes get heavy. "I don't need your help." He gets really sleepy. "I quit."

"Yo, are you okay?" Ángel asks. "You can't quit."

George struggles to keep his eyes open.

CP says to Ángel, "Your friend needs to slow down and open his heart. His brain will follow. My magical drink will help him get there."

"Cool. Can your magic drink make me a flying squirrel?"

"I got you, dude." CP dips another acorn cup into the steamy caldron and hands the drink to Ángel.

Ángel drinks. "It would be so neat to fly."

"Just like your friend," explains CP, "you must make the ultimate sacrifice. Only then will you be able to bridge the gap between you now and the animal you want to be."

"Sure, amigo. Whatever you say." Ángel laughs and suddenly falls asleep.

George tries to wake him. "Don't sleep. We've got to run away. Well, maybe just for a minute…" George finally succumbs to the drink and lays down to sleep.

CP spins a cocoon around George's sleeping body, working quickly from his feet up to his head.

George, sleeping inside the cocoon, mumbles to himself, "Oak Creek would be better off without me…" He falls into a deep sleep.

CHAPTER FIVE

Deep within a dream, George floats over the forest. From up high, the stunning landscape has a flowing creek and a waterfall just outside the tree line. As if he were a bird, George flies, dives down, and soars over the town center. It's a ghost town; no shops, cafes, or gyms. What happened? Where is everyone?

A flurry of butterflies swirl next to George. When they disperse, Ángel stands in their place.

"Ah! Where did you come from?"

Ángel speaks in a shaky ghost-like voice. "I come from the oaky drink with the zesty after taste."

"Why are you talking like that?" George asks.

Ángel drops the voice. "I'm trying to make an impression on your subconscious. Is it working?"

George shakes his head no.

"Maybe this will make an impression." Ángel snaps his fingers. Butterflies encase them, transporting them to George's tree house.

The butterflies disperse, leaving George and Ángel

floating above a scene of George and his Grannie, Greta, in the kitchen.

"Is that me?" George asks.

"Yes," Ángel says. "Do you remember this day?"

George watches as Greta walks to the kitchen table. She stumbles and falls. His former self helps her up. She asks him to grab her walker. He helps her up and onto her walker.

"I remember," George says. He watches himself sit at the table with Grannie.

"George, I need your help. Can you help me?"

"Of course, Grannie."

"I need you to run the bank for me," she says. George can't believe his ears.

"But you've always run the bank, and I'm... I'm not ready. I'm so young."

"I know, baby, but I'm getting old and you're the man of the tree house now. Oak Creek needs your help. I wouldn't ask if I didn't need your help."

George agrees, and she hands the ledger to him.

"Your ledger? But it's so important. I can't..."

"You must protect it at all costs. Can you do it?"

George shakes his head. "I don't know how. Only you can..."

Greta smiles. "We're in this together, George."

George clutches the ledger to his chest, and Greta gives him a big hug.

Ángel and George watch the memory unfold.

"I started running the bank the next day," George explains. "Grannie came to the bank less and less as the days went on. Eventually, she stopped coming at all."

"What if you hadn't said yes? Would Oak Creek be better off without you?" Ángel asks.

The butterflies encase them, and then they magically appear back on Main Street. George and Ángel find themselves in an empty town center. A nut falls from a tree and lands nearby. Mary, dressed in tribal clothes, pierces the nut with a spear while she carries the baby.

"Mary!" George calls out. He tries to hug her, but falls straight through her, creating a few butterflies that fly away.

"She can't hear you."

"Why not?" George asks. "What is she doing?"

An army of ants swarm Mary from all sides. She thrusts her spear to keep them at bay. They link arms to create a bully Mary's size, a phantom squirrel made of ants.

Ángel explains, "If you had never taken over the bank, there wouldn't be a way for everyone to work together to build up the community. It'd be every animal for themselves."

Mary throws her spear into the ants. A few pop out of formation, leaving a hole in its wake. The phantom ant squirrel pushes Mary. She falls back, clutching the baby. They break formation to swarm the nut. Mary throws the baby in the air, does a backflip, and smashes her spear into the nut, dispersing the ants. The baby falls back down, and she catches it.

"Whoa, she's good," George says.

Every ant turns toward Mary and leaps. The ants completely cover her and the baby. George calls out to Mary, but she can't hear him.

Greta appears out of nowhere with her walker, tribal paint on her face. She throws apple cores at Mary to get the ants off. One hits Mary in the face. "Ow!"

As Mary shakes ants off, Noel flies down and steals the nut. She jumps up and glides between trees. Chase swoops down and steals the nut from Noel's paws in mid-air. Noel falls, hitting each tree branch on her way down.

"Savage," Ángel says.

"But I took over the bank. So that means this isn't real. Take me back to the Oak Creek I know and love," George demands.

"You're the boss." Ángel snaps his fingers again, and the butterflies fly in.

When the butterflies fly away again, George and Ángel stand in the Oak Creek town center of today. The city looks bleak and without color. Christmas cheer is non existent. The town animals wait in line for nut rations. The ants stand on guard. Under Maddy's watchful eye, Tony gives each animal the bare minimum of food to eat.

Mary, carrying the baby, steps up to receive her portion. Maddy grabs the nuts from Tony and addresses Mary. "Dear Mary, welcome to the Ant Creek Bank. I'm so glad you're with us."

"Oh! Well, um… I'm still with George and the Oak Creek Bank," Mary says.

"Standing by him even after he abandoned you?" Maddy asks. "How embarrassing."

George floats overhead, watching. He struggles to glide to the ground. As soon as his feet touch down, he floats back up. "Mary! I'm here! Don't take that deal."

No one hears George.

Instead of handing the rations to Mary, Maddy skips her and gives them to Rabbit. "I'm terribly sorry everyone, but the Ant Creek Bank is now closed for the day." Maddy snaps her fingers, and the ants remove the stash in an instant. Mary is left empty-handed.

"Maddy, please! My family needs…"

The ants whisk Maddy away. Animals who didn't get a ration groan.

George calls out, "Don't worry, Mary. I'll make everything right."

Mary walks away, sad. She passes Noel and her brother Junior. Noel says, "I'm sorry, Junior. There won't be a Christmas this year. We barely have enough for dinner." Junior cries, exposing his missing tooth. George watches on with sadness.

Woodpecker sits on a branch up above. He shouts down, "Breaking news. Worst Christmas ever!" He drills into the side of the tree, creating a huge hole. The chipmunk with the deep voice pops out of the hole and yells, "Hey!"

The ant police intervene and arrest Woodpecker. George balls up his fists in frustration. He hates to see his friends treated this way.

Big Burly leaves with his ration. George tries to talk to him. "We've got to do something before Christmas comes. Maybe we can organize a team forage or…"

Big Burly walks away without hearing George. He meets up with his twenty squirrel children. He breaks one seed into twenty tiny little pieces.

Chase jets past, flying directly through George. A few butterflies disperse.

"This sucks," Chase says. "What ever happened to treat yo self? Especially during the holidays."

"Hey!" George yells. "Why can't anyone see or hear me? Make them hear me!"

Ángel says, "No can do. You left Oak Creek. You no longer have a care in the world. No nuts to forage. No bank to save. This is what it's like without you watching out for everyone."

"I don't like it."

"It's loco how many lives one squirrel touches. When

he's nut around, he leaves an awful hole."

"Get me out of here," George says.

A swarm of butterflies engulf him. As the butterflies disperse, George finds himself in the town center at night. A million ants crawl over everything.

"Why are we still here?" he asks Ángel.

"We're in the future, amigo. We're time traveling squirrels! How cool is that?"

"I hope things are better in this timeline."

"Define better…" Ángel says as George looks around the town overrun with ants. They burrow tunnels into the trees, causing extreme decay. The Oak Creek sign now reads "Ant Creek."

"Where's Mary?" George asks.

Ángel snaps his fingers, and the butterflies take them to Maddy's anthill. She stands outside her palace, protected by guards. George and Ángel float over the scene.

Mary approaches with the baby. Chester and Lester trail behind, tired and dragging their feet. Their clothes are tattered.

"You're late," Maddy says to Mary.

"I traveled far to forage enough for this month's payment." Mary lays several berries, nuts, and seeds at Maddy's feet. She bows before the queen.

"I'm afraid we must impose a late fee," Maddy says coldly. Mary pleads with her. The evil ant queen says, "We sympathize with your plight. We do. Therefore, your late fee will be added to next month's rent."

"I can't keep up."

"Oh, dear. Then we must seize your home. There are many ants ready to take your place."

Chester and Lester cry.

Mary asks Maddy, "How many more of us will be left

homeless this month?"

Maddy's eyes light up with anger. "How dare you speak to your Queen that way! Take your petty forage and go. You're no longer welcome here."

Mary cries. "I'm sorry, my Queen."

George tries to comfort Mary. "It's okay. I'm here."

"You're nut here," Ángel reminds him. "You left, remember?"

Mary runs into the forest with her brothers. George, floating, turns to follow Mary. He's suddenly faced with Greta in her walker.

"Ah! How does she keep doing that?"

Greta turns and ever so slowly follows Mary.

George floats after them and watches as Mary burrows underground with the kids and Greta in tow.

"Can we go home?" Lester asks.

"We'll make a new home here, together," Mary says.

"How am I supposed to crawl down there with my bad back?" Greta asks. "Pft!"

A mole pops out of the ground and yells, "This spot's taken!"

The baby cries. Mary clutches her brothers.

Ángel says to George, "You really had a wonderful life. Don't you see what a mistake it would be to throw it all away?"

"Yes! Get me back! Oak Creek needs me. Mary, I'm coming back! I'll make everything right again, I promise!"

"Very well then. Cashew later!" Ángel smiles and turns into a swarm of butterflies.

CHAPTER SIX

Back in CP's hut, the caterpillar does yoga. Two large cocoons hang overhead. One of them stirs. CP goes into downward facing dog. One cocoon falls from the ceiling and lands on his antenna. CP tries to move, but he's stuck under the weight of the cocoon. "Gah!"

George screams from inside the cocoon. "Get me back! I need to make it better." He nibbles a hole in the cocoon and wiggles his way out.

He looks around the empty hut. "Ángel? CP? Where is everyone?"

George hears CP struggling under the cocoon, so he lifts it off the caterpillar's antenna.

"Hey, CP. That was a wild ride!"

"Do you still think Oak Creek is better off without you?" CP asks.

"No, Oak Creek needs me. I know what I have to do now. I have to confront the bear!" George walks to the door with purpose.

"You seem ready to slay! Get it, George!"

George nods and opens the door. He pauses, then turns around with a nervous look. Before George can think twice, CP pushes him out the door.

Outside, a light snow dusts the ground. George licks his finger and tests the air. "If I were a bear, where would I live?" He looks left, right, back, then walks forward through the brush.

Chase calls down to George from overhead. "George, is that you?" He flies down from the sky.

"Chase! You can see me? You can hear me?" George shakes Chase and hugs him a little too tightly.

"Where have you been?" Chase asks. "You've been gone for two days. Mary's looking for you."

"Two days?! That drink was something else!"

"What drink?" Chase asks.

"Never mind that. Do you know where the big bad bear lives?"

"Why? What are you planning to do, George?"

"I'm going to confront the bear!"

Chase can't believe it. George tells Chase that he doesn't have a choice. Someone has to save Oak Creek! Chase agrees with that statement. He tells George that things have gotten pretty bleak since he left. "I might leave for the winter."

"But you always spend Christmas in Oak Creek, Chase."

"You should head home, George. They need you there."

George clutches his ledger to his chest and says, "I know."

Chase nods and flies away. George knows he can't go home until he's confronted the bear, so instead of going home, carries on with his mission.

Through the next tree line, he hears the roar of a waterfall. He stops to think. George remembers Big Burly talking to him in the bank. He said the bear's growls were louder than the waterfall. George listens to the waterfall echoing from the forest. The bear must live by the waterfall!

George heads that way. He soon hits a fork in the road and sniffs the air. On the left, lemon trees line a dark, thorny path. On the right, the path looks smooth and inviting. "Those lemons sure smell zesty. Aha!"

George remembers CP talking in his hut. He said, "I've searched the forest for that perfect zest. The lemon trees that mark the path toward the waterfall were the missing ingredient to make the recipe really sing." George nods his head, knowing.

"The lemon trees mark the path toward the waterfall. Big bad bear, here I come!" George takes the thorny path. Although it will be difficult, he knows it is the right way.

The terrain is rocky and hard to climb. He loses his footing and falls backward. George clutches the ledger to his chest, takes a deep breath, and carries onward. The sound of the waterfall grows louder. He must be getting close.

The tree line breaks, revealing a clear blue river. At the mouth, an epic waterfall crashes down. It's so pretty. George walks down the creek toward the waterfall.

"Now, if I were a bear, where would I be?"

Up ahead, a frog sits on a rock. George runs over to greet her. "Excuse me, dear Frog. Do you know where I can find a bear around here?"

The frog looks blankly at George and says, "Ribbit."

"Ribbit? Is that a town near here?"

"Ribbit."

"I don't speak your language," explains George. "Do you understand me? I'm looking for a bear."

"Ribbit. Ribbit."

"Okay. Thanks any way." George walks away.

A second frog joins the first. "What did he want?"

The first frog says, "He's looking for the bear."

"Did you tell him where to go?"

"No. I played dumb," says the first frog. "I didn't want to see a good squirrel get hurt. Ribbit!" The frogs high-five each other.

George stumbles over rocks near the mouth of the creek.

"Silly frog," he says to himself. "I'm definitely not in Oak Creek anymore. Stay sharp, George."

Just then, he slips and falls. His face lands next to a big rock with gashes in it. He remembers Woodpecker talking about the bear.

Woodpecker said, "It's a hundred feet tall with fangs that can break rock."

George picks himself up and walks up a rocky ravine. "I bet the bear lives in a rocky cave. If he can eat rocks, he should leave our nuts alone. How will I convince him of that?"

George practices his pitch as he climbs the rocks. "Excuse me bear, may I interest you in some rocks? I'll trade you for our nuts."

He shakes his head. "No, that won't work… Dear bear, if you give me the nuts back, I won't report you to the forest gods. You don't want to wind up in the nuthouse."

George rolls his eyes and screams out, "Ángel, you're rubbing off on me!" He tries again. "Dear bear…"

George walks up to the opening of a deep, dark cave. A

loud growl greets him from within. Fear takes over.

George gulps and whispers to himself, "Dear bear, please don't eat me."

CHAPTER SEVEN

George slowly enters the dark cave. He gulps as he passes the skeleton of a small animal. He kicks a rock, which tumbles down deeper into the shadows. It makes a loud sound. He pauses. No response from any bear within.

George continues with caution. "Maybe the bear is sleeping, and I can take the nuts back. It's not stealing if they were ours to begin with."

A growl trembles from within the cave, stopping George in his tracks. "Nope. Definitely not asleep."

George turns on his heels to leave, but pauses. "Pull yourself together. They need you." He takes a deep breath, turns around, and keeps going. Each step is slow and calculated. There's light up ahead.

George sees a few nuts near a big rock. He hides to scope the scene. He sees a huge brown bear sitting next to a fire. A few nuts litter the ground.

"Here goes nothing," George says to himself. He ignores his fears and shouts, "Hey you!"

George's shadow plays across the cave's wall, making him appear much bigger. The bear scratches and growls at the shadow.

"Ah! Who are you? What do you want?" the bear asks.

George's shadow speaks. "I'm here to collect."

"Collect?" asks the bear. "Do you collect rocks or something?"

The bear scratches at the shadow again and realizes she's touching the wall. She turns around and sees George as he really is. She screams with surprise.

George protects his head with his paws. "Please don't hurt me."

The bear leans down to check George out. Her snout gets close to him, and her breath blows through his fur.

"Aw, you're so cute!" the bear says.

"Cute?" Shocked, George slowly lowers his arms. "Thank you?"

The bear says, "I'm Betty. What's your name?"

"I'm George... and I'm here to collect." George puffs his chest out to seem bigger than he is.

Betty the bear laughs. "Yeah, you said that already. You must have a pretty extensive rock collection if you've got to come here to find new ones."

"Don't play dumb with me. How dare you steal from us! Just because you're bigger?"

"Excuse me?" Betty asks.

George softens. "Consider the rest of the forest animals! We're in this together."

"What do you mean? I would never steal from anyone," Betty says.

"You stole nuts from the Oak Creek bank." He picks up a nut from the ground and shows her. "See?"

Betty leans down and sniffs the nut. She sneezes, which

comes with an epic growl.

George flies back from the sheer velocity of the sneeze. He hits his head on a rock. "Ow!"

Betty says, "Whoops. My bad." She sniffles and wipes her nose with her paw. "I can't shake this cold. It's so annoying. I've had it ever since I moved into my new cave."

George picks himself up and walks back toward Betty. "I like what you've done with the place," he says.

"Yay! Thanks. I still have some decor ideas, but it works for now."

George smiles at Betty. He didn't expect her to be so nice.

"So you didn't steal our nut stash?" he asks.

Betty shakes her head. "I don't even like nuts. Hurts my tummy, if you know what I mean."

"Then why have you been terrorizing our foraging missions all season?"

Betty lays back with her paw over her forehead like a damsel in distress. "Ugh! First my fellow bears and now this?"

George comes closer and asks, "What's wrong?"

Betty explains. "I usually hibernate for the winter, but I can't sleep because of this cold. My constant sneezing drove all my friends away. Sounds like I'm scaring the entire forest."

"So you're all alone?"

She nods sadly.

"No one should be alone for Christmas," George says.

"I usually sleep through the holidays."

"Well, now that you're up, experience the best holiday of the year. The streets of Oak Creek are always so beautifully decorated. We have a big feast. We sing and open presents. It's the best day of the year!"

Betty smiles. "That sounds really nice. Let me check my calendar. Guess what? I'm free! Let's go! I could use a party right about now."

"If you didn't steal the nuts, then… It really is my fault." George looks up at Betty with guilty eyes.

"What's wrong, little fella?" she asks.

"I can't go home and face everyone after what I've done."

"Who wouldn't forgive a cute little squirrel like you? No matter what you've done." Betty nudges George to cheer him up. "You're pretty brave, you know that?"

George smiles. No one's ever said that to him before.

"It took a lot of guts to come in here. You'll need a lot of bravery to admit to your friends that you messed up. But you can do it."

Betty gets up and walks toward the cave opening. George doesn't stir. "Come on, let's go clear my name. I can't have the whole forest thinking I'm a mean bear!"

George still isn't sure. His friends and family will be angry when they find out he forgot to lock the bank.

"What are you waiting for? Isn't it almost Christmas?" Betty asks.

George checks his ledger and holds it close to his chest. "Yes, it's almost Christmas, and I'll be coming home empty-handed."

"That's okay, little fella. I'm the life of the party. I'll help you make everything right."

George reluctantly follows Betty out of the cave.

They walk back to Oak Creek together, getting to know each other. Betty is happy to have a new friend to talk to. It surprises George how friendly she is. He hopes to at least calm Oak Creek's fear of bears.

As they arrive just outside the town, George stops. He

realizes he can't go marching into town with a bear. First, he will have to warn everyone that Betty is coming. So they come up with a plan.

He covers Betty with bushes and says, "Once I give the signal, you can come out to meet everyone."

"Right, I'll pop out when you say Merry Christmas!" Betty pops her head out from behind the leaves with a toothy grin.

"Maybe with a little less fang exposed," George says.

Betty purses her lips. "Resting bear face? Like this?"

"A little more friendly," George says.

Betty gives a strained smile without showing teeth.

"That's... good. Great. Everyone's going to love you..." George doesn't sound so sure.

"I hope so," Betty says with a tight smile.

George laughs nervously and runs through the trees. He walks through the empty town center. When he passes the Oak Creek sign, he gives it a hug. There's still time! He heads toward the anthill.

George runs up to the elaborate palace to find Maddy passing out rations to the town. Everyone is there to get a few nuts, whatever Maddy will spare.

When Maddy sees George running up she says, "Well, well, well. Look who the bear dragged in."

"George!" Mary calls. George hugs Mary and his brothers, Chester and Lester. He even hugs grannie Greta.

"Where have you been?" Greta asks.

"I've been to see the bear."

A collective gasp from the town. George addresses everyone. "I have good news, folks! Betty is really nice."

"Betty?" Maddy asks.

"Betty the bear. She's not out to get us or our nuts! She didn't..."

"Fake news!" Maddy screams. "That bear is a menace! She's ruined the foraging season and robbed the bank." There's confusion amongst the townspeople.

"No, she didn't!" George insists. "It's all a big misunderstanding."

"Tell that to the bank customers who have nothing left!" Maddy yells.

George pulls out his ledger and says, "I know. But with the bear threat gone, we still have a little time to forage before Christmas!"

Betty leaps out from the trees, half covered in leaves. She screams, "Merry Christmas!"

Shock sweeps over the town.

"George, what have you done?" Maddy asks. "Bringing this beast to our doorstep!"

To Betty, Maddy's yells sound small and distant. She leans over to get a better look at the queen ant. She sniffs Maddy's ant hill and immediately sneezes!

To the Oak Creek animals, Betty's sneeze is loud and comes with a big, scary growl.

Maddy yells, "Everyone, run for your lives!" The townspeople scream and run in every direction.

The chipmunk with the high voice screeches, "Eek!" while the chipmunk with the deep voice says, "Oh my!"

George tries to yell over everyone. "Please, wait! You don't understand!" No one can hear George amongst all the yelling and running. Mary protects her younger brothers from the stampede of animals running in every direction.

The Old Squirrel shouts, "Stampede!" and pees his pants.

Betty asks George, "What's going on? They don't like me, do they?" She jumps up and down, scared of all the little animals running around.

Betty's jumps shake the ground, causing animals to fall over and cry.

Greta falls onto her back with her walker on top of her. Her legs run in place.

George drops his ledger. Betty accidentally smashes it with her feet. Pages from the important book explode into the air and fly away.

"Oh, no!" George calls out as he scrambles after the lost pages. He can only grab one page.

Maddy screams at George, "Look what you've done! Leave town before you make everything even worse."

George holds the only remaining page of the ledger to his chest. He watches the turmoil he's caused all around him. He really has made things worse.

Betty calls out, "George, let's get out of here."

George jumps on Betty's back, and they race through the trees together.

Mary calls after George, but he doesn't hear her.

Still stuck on her back, Greta says, "George ruined the ledger! How could he be so careless? The bank is ruined now…"

CHAPTER EIGHT

Betty runs full speed through the woods, knocking into trees. Her feet stomp the ground, sending shock waves through the forest. CP's hut shakes as they pass by.

Inside, Ángel's cocoon sways above CP, comes unlatched, and falls onto the caterpillar's head. His antenna are stuck underneath the cocoon again.

"I've got to find a better place to hang these things," CP mumbles to himself.

The cocoon jumps off CP's antenna and jiggles around until a paw crashes through the wrapping. Another paw pops out, then two feet and a tail. Finally, Ángel's head tears through the cocoon. He wears the rest of it like armor around his torso.

Ángel burps and says to CP, "Hey amigo, got any nuts? I'm hungry." He looks around and then asks, "Where is George?"

CP explains that George went to confront the bear. Ángel's jaw drops to the floor.

"No manches?! I gotta find him before he gets eaten. Cashew later!"

Ángel runs out of the hut. CP dips an acorn cup into his cauldron and takes a sip. He nods with approval.

"This drink really does taste zesty!"

Outside the hut, Ángel rushes through the trees, still wearing the cocoon around his torso. He runs into Betty's leg. He looks up at the massive bear towering over him. Ángel gasps, and his eyes bulge out of his head.

George says, "It's okay, Ángel. She's with me."

Ángel doesn't hear George. "Run, amigo! Run!" He turns and runs, hits a tree, and passes out. George rolls his eyes.

Betty says to George, "Hate to break it to you, but your friends are kinda mean. Like, this is the town you were raving about? I don't see it."

George apologizes. "It's not usually like this. Everyone in Oak Creek has a good heart. They're just in a bad place right now."

Betty asks what they can do to make it better, and George shrugs his shoulders.

"I honestly don't know what to do. I thought I could make things right, but maybe Oak Creek really is better off without me."

Ángel gets up. He points at Betty, scared speechless.

George says, "Yes, she's a bear. And no, she doesn't want to eat you."

Ángel cautiously walks past Betty to get to George. His teeth chatter with fear. "Are... are you sure it's safe?"

"Pretty sure," says George.

Ángel grabs George by the shoulders and shakes him. "Blink twice if you need saving, amigo."

"Calm down, Ángel. I confronted Betty about stealing

our nuts, but she didn't do it."

Betty nods. "I don't even like nuts."

George whispers to Ángel, "Gives her tummy troubles, if you know what I mean." Ángel crinkles up his nose in disgust.

George explains, "We went to town to clear her name, and everyone freaked out."

"So rude," Betty adds.

"It didn't help that she sneezed," George says. "She's had a cold ever since she moved into her new cave. Her sneezes have been scaring all the foragers."

Ángel flutters his eyes at George. "Remember what to do if you need saving."

George shakes his head. "Betty and I are going to stay here. Why don't you go to Nick's? You seem to enjoy distracting people with a trip to his place."

"I do like to hang with the homies, but it can wait," says Ángel. "This is important."

George says, "If Betty didn't steal the nuts, then we need to find out who did."

"Who could break into a locked bank?" Ángel asks. "Would they need to be an expert locksmith or something?"

George yells, "Forget about the locked door, okay? Everyone's a suspect. Assume anyone could walk right in."

Ángel and Betty look at George, surprised at his reaction. He seems really upset at any mention of the bank's door lock.

George lowers his voice. "We have to solve the mystery. If we think anyone could have come in, then we won't overlook a more important clue."

"Let's do this!" Ángel exclaims. A beat later, he asks, "How do we do this?"

"We investigate," says George.

"I'm in!" Betty says.

Ángel looks at Betty and asks, "Are you trying to steal my best friend?"

George tells Ángel to focus. He pulls out the last remaining page from his ledger. It's a map of Oak Creek.

It shocks Ángel to see the ledger ruined. "Oh no, your book! The whole town's savings! Without that book, no one will trust the bank."

"I know… I've lost the only record," George says sadly. He holds the page close to his chest and then lays it out in front of them. "I have to make things right." They all lean in to examine the map for clues.

***

Meanwhile, back in town, the animals gather, still shaken from seeing the bear. Maddy snaps her fingers and hundreds of ants link arms, creating a platform with their bodies to lift her up. Mary sees a ripped page from George's ledger. She picks it up, but the chilly wind blows it from her paw.

Maddy says to everyone, "That bear has scared Oak Creek for too long. We cannot wait for it to strike again. We must protect ourselves."

"Yeah!" shouts Tony.

The chipmunk with the deep voice says, "Hey, that's my line!"

"Our lives are at stake," continues Maddy. "We have to keep the bear out. We must build a wall to protect Ant Creek."

No one notices Maddy changed the name of the town. Big Burly points out that a wall would have to be huge to keep a bear out. Bears are very tall, after all.

Maddy says, "We may be small, but we are mighty. Just look at what the many can do." The ant platform she stands on grows taller. The animals aren't sure if they should clap or fear Maddy. She tells everyone what to do.

"The beavers will chop the wood. Squirrels will carry it. The birds will help us reach new heights."

"Birds are great, aren't we?" asks Chase. Noel hits Chase on the arm and rolls her eyes. She walks away and finds Mary in the crowd as Maddy says, "We work day and night until it's done. If we don't, we will perish!"

Noel whispers to Mary, "This doesn't feel right."

Mary agrees. "Who put Maddy in charge?" she asks. "And why would we build a wall when we need to be foraging for nuts?"

Maddy says to her ant soldiers, "If George is found anywhere near Oak Creek, arrest him!" Tony and the soldier ants nod and bow down to their queen.

Mary and Noel both know George would never do anything to hurt the town. He loves Oak Creek.

"What should we do?" Noel asks Mary.

"We have to help George. You're not afraid of a little adventure, are you?" Mary asks.

Noel gulps.

Mary has a light in her eyes. She's been wanting to help her family for a long time. Now is her chance!

***

George and Ángel look through the ransacked bank, looking for clues. They're looking for something, anything, to help them find out who stole the stash from the bank. Ángel finds a nut under some papers. He picks it up and puts it in the cocoon armor still around his torso.

From outside, Betty asks, "Any luck in there?"

George and Ángel walk out of the bank, and Betty peeks out from behind the tree. She says, "I see a lot of activity down by the anthill over there. They're up to something big."

"Who stole the stash from the bank?" George must find a clue soon.

Betty points and says, "We should get out of here. Soldier ants at three o'clock."

Ángel nods toward the approaching soldier ants as Betty hides behind the tree. Her face is still very visible.

Snow falls. George licks his finger and checks the air. He holds his empty hands to his chest without his ledger.

***

Back at the anthill, the town works tirelessly to build a stick wall. Big Burly hoists a tall pointy stick up. Chase catches it from above, and they work together to secure its position on the wall. More snow falls.

Maddy yells at everyone. "Higher, higher, higher! High enough to keep the bear out."

Big Burly asks, "Maddy, shouldn't we be building the wall around the whole town? Not just around the anthill?"

"We have to start somewhere," she says. "Stop dilly dallying and we'll get to it before Christmas."

Nick the spider taps Maddy on her shoulder. She turns around and says to him, "I have a very special job for you. Check in with the colony and they'll get you started." Nick nods and heads into the anthill.

Chase glides down from the tree and asks Maddy if he can take a break. "How about some of those delicious nuts you have somewhere around here, Maddy? I'm hungry."

Maddy whispers to Chase, "Birds have such special talents. Perhaps an extra ration just for you?"

Chase smiles. "I am pretty special, aren't I?"

Noel watches them from a tree branch above. Then she glides on her wing flaps, down toward Mary, who ties sticks together with other animals.

"Any intel from above?" Mary asks Noel.

"Not really. Chase is bragging about how special he is. You know, the usual. I'm not very good at this, Mary."

Mary tells Noel she's doing great, and then adds, "Isn't it strange how no ants are working on the wall?"

Noel looks around. Only a few soldier ants protect the ant hill entrance.

"You're right, Mary. Where'd they all go?"

"I think they're inside the anthill. We've got to get in there to see what's going on."

Noel shakes her head. "They have the front door protected. How can we get inside?"

"I'll see if I can get in through the back door," Mary says. Noel tells Mary to be careful. Mary nods and slinks toward the back of the anthill. She hides behind a stack of sticks so no one will see her.

When the coast is clear, Mary tiptoes toward the back door of the anthill. She finds a soldier ant nibbling on a stick.

The soldier ant sees Mary and asks her what she is doing back there. Mary lies and says she's looking for more wood to build the wall. The ant points to a stack of sticks. Mary is not paying attention. Instead, she tries to see what's going on inside the anthill. She sees Tony passing nuts out of the anthill in an assembly line. They're moving a lot of nuts out... She wants to get a closer look, so she hides behind a nearby tree.

The soldier ant taps Tony on the shoulder and tells him to take a 5 minute break. Tony sighs and passes a heavy nut to the soldier ant.

"Boy, this is a lot of work," Tony says. "Do you think we'll ever get a day off? My request for holiday vacation got denied again. The Queen has never been richer, and all we get is more unpaid overtime."

The soldier ant agrees, but says, "The Queen knows what's best, right?" The ant assembly line continues passing the epic stash out of the anthill.

Mary pops up from behind the tree. She crawls toward the anthill without being seen. Once she's close, she runs to the back door. The soldier ant sees her run inside and yells at the other ants. "Grab her!"

Tony turns around, surprised to see a swarm of his fellow ants leaping onto Mary. They take her down in front of him. Oh no, the ants caught Mary!

CHAPTER NINE

George, Ángel, and Betty stare at the map of Oak Creek. Snow falls onto the page.

George mumbles, "Who could have stolen the stash? Think, George, think."

Ángel says, "All this thinking is making me hungry. Let's eat." He pulls out the nut he found in the bank. He holds it out for George. "Here, amigo. Have a bite."

George shakes his head. "I don't have time to eat."

Ángel holds the nut out to Betty. "How about you, Betty bear? Want a snack?"

Betty sniffs the nut and recoils. She holds back a sneeze. "Ahh... ahh... ahh choo!" Betty sneezes with a growl.

The thrust of her sneeze sends Ángel flying backward. Stars circle his pulsing head.

"I take it you're not a health nut," jokes Ángel.

George takes the nut from Ángel's hand. "Betty, you haven't sneezed in a while. Smell the nut again for me."

George sets the nut on the ground in front of Betty. She bends down and sniffs it. A sneezing fit ensues. Ángel covers his head from the sheer velocity of the sneezes. When she's done, Ángel drips with snot.

"Today's nut my day," says Ángel.

Betty wipes her nose. "Ugh, I thought my cold was getting better."

"Betty, don't you see? You don't have a cold. You're allergic to nuts!" George exclaims.

"I am?!"

George tells her to smell the nut one more time to make sure. Ángel braces himself. Betty smells the nut and sneezes.

Betty says, "OMG George, you're right! I'm allergic to nuts! Wow. This explains so much!"

Ángel tells George he's a genius for figuring that out.

"Figuring it out..." George mumbles to himself, thinking. He remembers Betty sniffing Maddy's anthill. That's what caused her to sneeze in town.

George thinks back to when he saw the ransacked bank. Standing in the center of the chaos was Maddy. She was smiling as she stood in the empty bank. George's eyes grow wide. He's figured it out.

"Maddy! The anthill!" George says.

Ángel asks if Maddy is allergic to nuts, too.

"No, Ángel. Maddy robbed the bank. The stash is in the anthill. We have to get it back. We have to save Christmas!"

Betty and Ángel are ready to help, but George tells them to stay where they are. "If we all go, they'll see us. I'm going to sneak into the anthill to find the stash. Once I do, I'll signal you for backup."

Betty says they need a better signal this time. "Merry

Christmas was too confusing last time." George agrees.
***

Back at the anthill, Maddy watches the animals build her wall. She yells at them, "Faster! Higher! Don't stop now!"

Chase places a stick on the wall with great effort. When Maddy calls him, he sighs and flies down to the ground. "Where's my extra special ration, Maddy? I'm doing the work of ten squirrels."

Maddy whispers, "Be a good bird and keep an eye out for intruders from up there, will you?"

Chase folds his wings. "No snack, no work."

Maddy nods to one of her soldier ants, and they toss Chase a seed. "Now get back to work!" she yells.

Chase is sick of being yelled at. He tosses the seed and flies away. He's done working for Maddy.

Maddy yells at her ants to move faster. Out of the corner of her eye, she spots a squirrel's tail hiding behind a log. She watches George sneak toward the anthill.

"Arrest that squirrel!" Maddy yells and points to George. She sees him, so he comes out of hiding and runs as fast as he can.

The ant army chases George. He grabs some leaves, crumbles them, and throws the dust in their eyes. The first row falls back, but more follow.

The ants catch up, jump onto George, and he falls. They tie his hands together with webbing, carry him to Maddy, and lay him at her feet.

***

Back in the forest, Betty and Ángel pace. They hope

George is okay. They want to help, but are waiting for the signal.

Ángel says, "I'd go check on George, but I don't want to make him mad."

Betty adds, "I'd probably just sneeze all over and make things worse."

Chase flies over, surprised to see them together. "Say what?! Ángel, what are you doing with the big bad bear?"

"Excuse me? Who are you calling big?" Betty asks. "How rude!" She sucks her stomach in.

Ángel says, "She's on our side, amigo."

Chase shrugs his bird shoulders. "I don't know, I just spent all day building a stupid wall to keep her out."

Ángel asks Chase how Noel is doing.

"What are you gonna do, go save her from the teeny tiny little ants? You're not even a flying squirrel. You're basic." Chase laughs.

Ángel says, "Those ants are evil, man. And yeah, maybe I will go help Noel, because I'm nut basic." He puffs out his chest beneath the cocoon armor and walks toward town.

Betty grins and leans in towards Chase, licking her lips. "Now that you're alone with the big bad bear, you better watch your back, buddy."

Chase is unfazed. Since Chase is not scared of her, Betty drops the act.

"How do you stay so chill?" she asks. "What's your secret?"

Chase looks around to make sure no one is listening. He leans in and says, "I fake it."

"You do?" Betty asks.

Chase says in a panic, "Oh yeah. I'm losing it inside right now. If George doesn't save Christmas, I have to fly south for the winter. I don't want to do that! I like Oak Creek. Squirrels look up to me here. The other birds make fun of me, but here, I'm cool."

Betty tries to calm Chase down. He grabs her face and adds, "Those little ants totally freak me out!"

Betty pulls away. "Relax. How bad could they be?"

Out of nowhere, a huge net falls onto Betty. She's trapped! Lots of little ants jump down onto Chase. He screams, "Ahhhhhh!"

Betty tears a hole in the net with her claw. Nick the spider slides down and quickly repairs the hole. He spins another layer of web around Betty to seal her in tight. Betty's attempt to fight fails. She's caught in the web!

Back at the anthill, George lays at Maddy's feet with hands tied. Her soldier ants bring Mary out and put her next to George. She's tied up too. They're doomed!

CHAPTER TEN

George and Mary lay at Maddy's feet, tied up. George asks Mary what happened.

Maddy answers for her. "Mary broke into the anthill. George, you and your family have brought great suffering to Ant Creek."

"Don't you mean Oak Creek?" George asks.

"That's what I said. You must now face the consequences of your actions. I sentence you both to life in prison."

Noel chimes in from the sidelines. "You can't do that! They have the right to a fair trial."

Maddy tells Noel she's chosen the wrong team. She snaps her fingers, and her soldiers grab Noel and tie her up as well. The animals stop working and gather to watch.

George says, "You won't get away with this, Maddy. I know the truth. I know you stole the stash from the bank. And I can prove it."

Gasps from the crowd. Is George telling the truth?

Maddy laughs. "We've done no such thing. How undignified."

George tells the town, "Maddy has stolen our stash. She wants to take your homes. And now she's enslaved you to build a wall to keep the bear out. But the bear isn't the problem."

Maddy yells, "Silence! Ants, take him away."

Big Burly yells, "Let George speak!"

The crowd shouts out in agreement.

The chipmunk with the deep voice says, "Yeah!"

George continues. "The stash must be hidden in her palace. Open the anthill up to us, Maddy. Show us what's inside."

The animals pick up sticks and point them at Maddy. They chant, "What's inside? What's inside? What's inside?"

Mary whispers to George, "I think they're moving the stash to a new location."

George can't hear Mary over the chanting.

Maddy laughs. "Too little too late, dear George. You don't know what you're up against."

Giant wings flip out of Maddy's back, revealing that she's a flying ant! Her group of soldier ants also unleash their wings. They slowly rise into the air.

Maddy says, "You fools are no match for my army. Get 'em boys!"

Maddy laughs as her swarm of flying ants grabs George, Mary, and Noel by the fur. The ants fly them through the forest, following Maddy's lead. The other animals watch on in horror.

Ángel pops his head out of a nearby bush as the flying ants carry his friends away. He runs after them.

The flying ants take George, Mary, and Noel to a thin tree branch that dangles over a steep cliff. At Maddy's command, the flying ant army drops the gang onto the shaky tree branch, which wobbles under their weight. Maddy laughs as she watches them struggle to keep their balance.

Maddy asks her army if they are done moving the stash. A soldier ant reports, "Almost done, my Queen."

Maddy says to George and the gang, "We'd really love to stay and watch your fall, but there are more important things to attend to." She snaps her fingers and flies away. Most of her army follows, but some stay to chew through the branch holding George, Mary and Noel. They're in danger of falling over the cliff soon.

Ángel runs through the forest. He sees his friends on the breaking branch. It's going to snap at any moment!

Mary tries to say goodbye to George, but he says, "It's too early for goodbyes. Quick, chew through your binds." The squirrels chew through the webbing around their paws as they dangle above the cliff.

Ángel climbs up a nearby tree. He swallows his fear, jumps off the branch, and dives.

The ants eat through the wood branch, which shreds and buckles. Noel loses her balance and falls off!

Ángel flails his arms as he free falls. The cocoon around his torso rips off, revealing new wing-flapped arms. Ángel is now a flying squirrel! He glides gracefully through the air, swoops down into the edge of the cliff, and catches Noel. George and Mary watch, shocked.

"Ángel has wings!" George says with awe.

Ángel glides above the cliff and flies Noel to safety. He climbs back up a nearby tree, jumps off to save Mary. Ángel glides down to the ground with her next.

George frees his hand from the binds as the branch breaks and falls into the ravine.

"Ahhhhhhh!" George screams as he falls.

Ángel glides down and reaches over the cliff.

Mary and Noel clutch each other with fear. They can't lose George! They hope Ángel can save him.

George grabs onto Ángel's hand just in the nick of time. Ángel pulls him up to safety! Whew, that was a close one.

George says to Ángel, "Thanks, amigo."

Ángel says with tears in his eyes, "No, amigo... Tu eres mi familia."

George hugs Ángel and says, "You're right. We're family."

Noel joins in their hug. She asks Ángel, "Since when can you fly?"

Ángel flaunts his newfound wings. "My Christmas wish came true! It all started with a wise old caterpillar and an oaky drink with a zesty after taste."

George and Ángel laugh.

"Quick, let's get back to the anthill and find our stash!" George says. They all run back to Oak Creek together.

When they get back, there are no ants guarding the front door, so the squirrels enter the empty anthill.

Inside, little tunnels line the vaulted walls. A handful of ants charge at them, carrying pointy spears. Ángel and Noel jump up and hang onto the ceiling. George and Mary dodge the ant spears as they lunge toward them. Mary grabs George's hands and does a backflip over him, kicking a few ants. The ants fall back in a line like dominoes. George whips his tail around, taking out a row of ants. Mary smiles, impressed.

Ángel drops from the ceiling, taking out more ants. Only one ant remains. The squirrels strike battle poses.

The soldier ant drops his spear and says, "I don't get

paid enough for this."

George motions for him to leave. The ant runs away scared. Noel glides down, and they all walk through the grand hall.

Ángel says, "This place gives me the creeps."

George asks where everyone is. "There are thousands of ants in the colony. Only some of them flew away."

"Where did they fly to?" Mary asks.

They walk through to the back of the anthill, where they find Tony and a few ants passing what's left of the stash outside. Only a few nuts remain. Tony walks inside to pick up the last nut. He stops when he sees the squirrels.

George asks Tony, "Where is the stash?"

"Long gone," says Tony. "We've been moving it from one place to another all week."

Tony picks up the nut, and his back cracks. This is the most epic crack yet! He drops the nut and sits on it, moaning.

"Where is she taking everything?" George asks.

Tony says, "How should I know? I'm just a peasANT. She snaps, and we work. She doesn't stop to tell us the plan."

"That must make you mad," George says.

Tony nods. "You know what? It does. It's hard to see your Queen lying and stealing, but I'm just one ant. How should I know what's best for the colony? And what can I do about it?"

Mary asks Tony to help them find the stash.

Tony rubs his lower back, thinking. Finally, he says, "Follow the line of ants to the drop sight. Come on, I'll take you there." He leads the gang outside.

Tony, George, Ángel, Mary, and Noel run past a line of ants that pass nuts to a landing point at the creek. Falling snow dusts the ground as they reach the shoreline. There, Maddy and the flying ants float above twenty huge stash piles!

George says to Maddy, "Give it up, Maddy. It's the end of the line."

She laughs and says, "Dear George, this is the end… for you. For us, it's just the beginning."

Maddy snaps her fingers, and the ants fly down to grab webbed nets on the ground. They soar back up with the nets filled with nuts. Maddy snaps her fingers again, and the ants fly off with twenty full nets.

"We can't let them get away!" George whistles loudly. Nothing happens.

"Ángel, where's Betty?" George asks.

"I left her with Chase," he replies.

George runs and jumps onto one net in mid-air and holds on for dear life. "Ahhhhh!"

Tony says, "Take me with you!" He jumps onto George's tail as he's flown away on one of the stash nets. He climbs up George's tail and torso, and up to George's shoulder.

Ángel runs up a tree, jumps, and glides over to the next tree to chase the ants. Noel follows.

"There's no way I'm sitting this one out," Mary says. She runs to follow the stash down the river.

Chase flies overhead, panting. He sees George gripped onto one of the stash nets, surrounded by hundreds of flying ants. He passes out from the stress of it all.

Mary shakes and slaps Chase. He jolts awake.

"Pull yourself together!" Mary yells.

Chase says, "I'm not freaking out right now. Not at all!"

"Good," says Mary. "Let's go!"

Mary jumps onto Chase's back. They fly after the nuts.

CHAPTER ELEVEN

As Maddy and her ant soldiers fly the stash nets down the creek, she sees Ángel and Noel chasing from the sidelines. Ángel throws a stick through the swarm, knocking a few ants out of formation.

Maddy yells to her army, "Fly faster, you lazy dimwits. They're gaining on us!"

The net George clings to dips close to the creek. He holds his grip and lifts his feet to avoid the water. With great effort, he pulls himself up the net with Tony on his shoulder.

He says to Tony, "We have to get closer to Maddy. I'm going to jump."

Tony looks at the gap between the next net.

"Are you insane?" Tony asks.

George yells for Tony to hold on tight. He steadies himself as Tony grips his fur. George jumps onto the next net. Tony sighs with relief when they nail the landing.

The force of George's jump causes the ants to drop the previous net, losing their nuts in the water.

George looks back at the lost nuts with dismay. He calls out, "No nuts left behind!"

"I'm on it!" Noel yells from the trees. She turns around and goes after the lost nuts.

Chase and Mary fly toward Maddy, who yells for her swarm to fly faster.

Mary says to Chase, "Come on, let's take out some ants!"

"Of course that's what a confident bird like me would do." Chase swallows his fear and swoops downward. He flies through the swarm, knocking out rows of flying ants. A few stash nets fall into the water.

Chase lets out a blood-curdling scream as he rubs his head with his wing. "Ah! Get the ants off me! Eek!"

Mary rolls her eyes. "There are no ants on you. Just me."

"Cool, cool... In that case, let's do it again!" Chase doubles back and flies through the swarm again, thinning their ranks.

A large Ninja Ant jumps on a net close to George. He flashes a handful of wooden ninja stars. He throws them at George, one by one. "Waaaaa yaaaaaa!"

"Watch out!" Tony cries.

George crunches his body up and down to avoid the ninja stars. Tony is tossed around. The ninja stars keep coming.

George jumps off the net to avoid another star. He falls down and grabs onto the bottom of the net. His feet glide through the water. He climbs back up to the top of the net.

Scared, Tony grips George's face so tightly, George can't keep his eyes open. "Tony, I can't see!"

George shakes his head. Tony falls, but saves himself

by grabbing onto George's tail.

The Ninja Ant throws his last star. It cuts George's net in half, releasing the nuts into the water. The ants carrying the empty net let go. The net, with George and Tony on it, falls toward the creek below. George does a backflip through the air and lands onto another nearby stash net. Whew!

Tony says, "That was close!"

The Ninja Ant hasn't given up yet…

Ángel gains on the ants from the sideline. A swarm comes for him. He pulls out a pair of sticks and wields them like nunchucks. He knocks out a bunch of ants, but they keep coming. Several flying ants work together to push him off a branch. He grasps at the air and right before hitting the ground. He opens his wings and glides. Ángel flies to the next branch with a huge smile on his face. "Woo hoo! I love being a flying squirrel!"

As the chase gets closer to the waterfall, the snow picks up with a chilly burst of wind. Everyone works harder to fly against the blast, including Queen Maddy in the front of the pack. Water droplets from the waterfall turn into ice daggers that fall into the creek below.

The Ninja Ant jumps onto George's net. George whips his tail around, trying to knock off the Ninja. Tony is whipped around in the process.

The Ninja Ant karate-kicks George in the face. His body spins, and he's left dangling one-handed. Tony's life hangs in the balance as he grips to a lone lock of George's tail fur.

The Ninja Ant punches George several times. George regains both hands on the net. He whips the Ninja profusely with his tail, bringing Tony up into the mix. Tony slaps the Ninja Ant for good measure.

George kicks the Ninja, causing it to lose balance and fall into the water. That's the end of him!

Tony crawls up George's tail and settles back onto his shoulder. George jumps onto the next stash net, getting close to Maddy.

"Give us back our nuts, Maddy," George says.

"Bow down to your Queen, and I will show you mercy."

"Don't mess with Oak Creek!" George whistles, and his gang charges from all sides. Ángel glides in from the right. Chase and Mary fly in from the left. The ants have nowhere to go but through the waterfall.

Maddy laughs. She snaps her fingers, and a giant wooden catapult pokes out, parting the falling water.

"You're on my turf now," Maddy says.

More flying ants come out of the waterfall to join Maddy. Her army holds spears, ready to attack.

George fills with fear as the ants throw their spears at Chase and Mary. Chase flies erratically to dodge them.

Maddy and her army fly toward the waterfall.

Out of nowhere, there's a deep roar! Betty runs down the creek growling. Her paws stomp through the water at breakneck speed.

"No one puts Betty in a net," she says.

George smiles at the sight of Betty.

Maddy calls for her army to fall back. She flies into the parted waterfall, followed by the frontline of her army and the remaining stash nets.

The snow storm grows. Another large gust, and the waterfall freezes. The net George and Tony cling to enters the waterfall.

Chase and Mary continue to dodge spears in the air.

"Be careful, George!" Mary cries.

Betty reaches the waterfall as the final nut stash enters. She stands on hind legs to reach them, but it's too high. Frozen droplets fall down on her like daggers. She growls as she protects herself with her arm.

Maddy settles into a cave within the frozen waterfall. She's surrounded by her massive army of flying ants, the remaining stash nets, and the large wooden catapult.

Tony lets go of George, but stays close.

Maddy snaps her fingers, and half of her army fills the catapult with the remaining nuts while the other half threatens George with spears.

"You won't get away with this, Maddy," George says.

She laughs. "You never should have been in charge of the bank, George. You were just giving nuts away. And then you left the bank unlocked. What would your grannie think? Oak Creek depended on you, and you let everyone down."

Shock and guilt sweep over George.

"I'll tell everyone you left the bank unlocked," Maddy says. Her reflection in the ice looms over George.

Anger takes over George's face. His paws clench into fists.

"You're too much of a coward to hurt me," Maddy tells him.

"You're right, Maddy. That's not my style. And it was wrong of me to leave the bank unlocked. It was my job to protect the vault, and I failed."

"That's right," Maddy says. "You need to run away for good. Oak Creek is better off without you."

George holds his empty hands to his chest. "No! I'll tell the town it was my mistake. They deserve to know. But you're the one who took all the nuts. You tried to take over the town."

Maddy shrugs. "The wealth would trickle down someday."

George shakes his head. "It doesn't work like that. We're all connected. If some are suffering, all are suffering. Even though we're different, we need to look out for each other in order to survive... and thrive. We're in this together."

"How charming," she says with a laugh.

George says, "You will face trial for what you've done."

"Ha! I don't need Oak Creek! I'll create a new colony right here. My workers can build anything."

Maddy snaps her fingers and point at George. "Ants! Get rid of him."

Her army of ants move toward George slowly, tired. They've been working so hard to move the stash all over the forest.

George backs away, scared. The ice below him starts to crack.

CHAPTER TWELVE

Maddy's army slowly closes in on George in the frozen waterfall.

He pleads with Maddy. "Please. You don't have to do this."

Tony steps in front of George. The advancing ants halt. Tony says to his fellow ants, "It sounds like a lot of work to build a whole new colony. I like the one we have in Oak Creek."

"Who are you?" Maddy asks. "No one cares what you think."

Tony asks Maddy, "Are we all nameless playthings to you?"

He looks back at the other ants. "I don't know about you guys, but I'm sick and tired of doing her bidding. We're always working and building for her. When are we going to get a little time off to enjoy life?"

"Yes, of course," Maddy says.

Another soldier ant speaks up. "The Queen doesn't keep her promises. I'm with Tony. Come on guys, let's go home without her."

"What? You can't have a colony without a queen," Maddy says in shock.

"You're right," Tony says. "But we can have a democracy!"

The ants look at each other, thinking.

"Come on, what do you all say?" Tony asks. "Freedom! Freedom!" The ants join Tony in his chant. "Freedom. Freedom. Freedom!" The ants all cheer.

George says, "Good luck out there on your own, Maddy."

She replies, "If I'm going down, you're all coming with me."

Maddy flies up to the catapult. She turns it, aiming toward the frozen waterfall. She pulls the lever, releasing the remaining nut stash into the frozen wall.

"Good luck without me!" Maddy yells.

The ice structure cracks under the impact, causing it to break. Everyone braces for the fall. The floor drops underneath them, sending George, the nut stash, ice daggers, and all the ants into the creek.

Maddy tries to fly away, but she's knocked down by falling ice.

From below, Betty watches the ice fall down like knives. Mary, Chase, and Ángel hold their breath as the ice structure collapses. A large ice chunk falls, with George and the ants close behind.

Betty runs toward the falling debris, roaring. She head butts the ice dagger out of the way and moves her large body to catch George and the ants.

When they know they're safe on Betty's back, George and the ants cheer.

Snow falls. Betty walks out of the water toward the

shore. Ángel, Mary, and Chase cheer her on.

George and the ants jump off Betty's back. George hugs Mary and Ángel tight. A few animals from town run out of the trees to join; Big Burly, the chipmunks, Nick the spider, Rabbit...

"There you are! Is everyone okay?" Big Burly asks.

George clears his throat. "Guys, I have to tell you the truth. The night before the bank was robbed... I forgot to lock the door."

Chase says, "Smooth move."

Ángel hits Chase, so he adds, "I mean, hey... We all make mistakes."

Ángel steps up. "Oh, amigo. I distracted you. It's my fault, too."

"An honest mistake, George. I forgive you," Big Burly says.

Nick the spider approaches. "We've all made mistakes."

The chipmunk with the deep voice adds, "Yeah."

The chipmunk with the high voice says, "Uh-huh."

The animals gather in a tight circle around George.

"Thanks," he says, "but we're in trouble. We've lost everything. The entire stash is gone."

Noel breaks in carrying a net... only half full. "I tried to get as many as I could, but with the water and wind..." She shows what's left of the stash.

"That won't get us very far," George says.

Noel puts the nuts in the center of the circle. "Still, we'll share them equally. We're in this together, right George?"

George eeks out a small smile.

Big Burly steps up and adds a few nuts to the pile. "I had a few saved for a snowy day."

Rabbit hops in and drops a load of seeds. "I was saving

up for a new leg, but that can wait until next year. This one's still got a lot of luck left in it." Rabbit knocks on his fake leg.

Nick throws in some nuts with one of his spider legs. "It's not much, but I also have a lot of venom to share."

"That'll put legs on your chest!" George jokes.

Nick and George laugh. George pats one of Nick's legs, and the spider embraces him with all eight.

Some ants put nuts into the pile from the creek. Tony smiles through his back pain as he places a nut on the growing stash.

The chipmunks throw in some seeds. The one with the deep voice says, "You've always been good to us, George. We're all in this together."

The chipmunk with the high voice adds, "Yeah!"

Everyone laughs. George holds his empty hands to his chest, smiling with tears in his eyes. He looks at all the friendly faces around him.

Betty collects some nuts from the shoreline and pushes them into the pot. "There are no more pesky bears to hurt your foraging missions," she adds.

George hugs her snout. It's close to the nuts so she sneezes! The animals brace for it. Their fur blows in the wind.

"Oh my! Oh my!" George cries.

"What is it?" Mary asks.

"Betty, when did you say you started sneezing?" George asks.

"As soon as I moved into my new cave."

"That cave?" He points to her cave entrance near the waterfall.

"Yeah. It still needs some work, but do you guys all want a tour?"

George nods. "Do we ever! If you're allergic to nuts, then I'll bet the bank you're sitting on a gold mine!"

George climbs onto Betty's head, and she walks him toward the cave. He climbs up onto the roof. There, he finds the most epic nut stash lying right under an acorn tree. The animals join him one by one and cheer.

"This is going to be the best Christmas ever!" George exclaims. He passes nuts to Ángel, who passes it to Chase, who passes it to Tony… The full assembly line forms with both ants and animals working together.

***

Back in Oak Creek on Christmas day, the town has been restored to its full holiday glory. A circular table fills the town center with the Christmas tree in the middle. Everyone feasts on nuts, seeds, and fruitcake.

George looks around his town and smiles. Children run around laughing, ants co-mingle with animals, and Betty wears a Christmas hat.

Rabbit pops off his fake leg and hands it to Betty.

"Honestly, I already feel really lucky. Thanks though," Betty says to Rabbit.

Rabbit shrugs and pops his leg back in. Betty laughs.

Big Burly puts an acorn cup of almond milk with two paper straws in front of Tony and another soldier ant.

"Finally, some paid holiday time off!" Tony says.

"Cheers to that!" adds a soldier ant. The two ants grab their straws and drink up.

Noel greets Ángel with Junior. "Junior, I think we should give our friend here some flying lessons so he can really get far!"

"Hey little amigo. That'd be awesome," says Ángel.

Chase flies down and joins them. "I guess you're not a basic squirrel anymore, huh, Ángel?" Chase puts Ángel in a playful headlock.

"I never was!" Ángel says, wriggling out of Chase's grip. He flies circles around Chase, causing the bird to fall over.

Junior laughs, showing off his missing tooth. "Noel, can Ángel babysit instead of Chase?" he asks.

"Hey! I want to babysit," Chase says loud enough for everyone to hear. He blushes.

George laughs. CP flies out to greet George. The caterpillar is now a beautiful butterfly.

"Who needs a swaddle?" CP asks George. "Come here, give me some love." CP wraps George in a big hug with his wings then flies off, laughing.

George turns around and is faced with Greta in her walker, carrying the baby. "Ah! How do you keep surprising me like that, Grannie?"

Greta laughs and says, "You did good, kid. I'm sorry if I've been hard on you. I pushed because it was important for you to succeed. I think Oak Creek bank officially has a new owner, if you want."

"Thanks. I'd like that. I feel ready to be the boss."

"Merry Christmas, George," Greta says.

"Merry Christmas, Grannie!" George moves in to hug Greta, but she passes him the baby instead.

Mary comes over to George and Greta. She tells George she has a present for him.

"What else could I possibly need?" he asks.

Mary hands him a wooden box. Ángel, Noel, and all the animals watch as George opens the box. Inside is a brand new ledger. He gasps and clutches the book to his chest.

"Thank you. This means the world to me," he says.

"You mean the world to Oak Creek," Mary adds.

Everyone claps for George. He's so glad he told them the truth, and they love him anyway.

"You know," George says to Mary. "I could use help around the bank. What do you say, sis? Will you be my partner?"

Mary smiles and hugs George. "I'd love to help!"

Their younger brothers, Chester and Lester, come over and join the hug.

"Will you play with us, George?"

"Should we plan another bank heist?" George asks.

"I'm the banker!" shouts Chester.

"No, I'm the banker!" shouts Lester.

"I'll be the robber," George says. "I've had a little practice." George winks at Mary. She smiles.

"But the bad guy never wins," Mary reminds him.

George hands the baby back to Greta, and for a change, it spits up on her! She groans.

Old Squirrel Stewart approaches Greta, raising his eyebrows in greeting. Her shoulder is covered in spit-up, and his pants have a pee stain. They inch closer and hold hands, smiling.

George and Mary chase after Chester and Lester as the rest of the town sings Christmas songs. It really is the best Christmas ever!

MORE FROM JP CAWOOD

Check out these other children's book titles by JP Cawood:

Sam & The Secrets of the Universe: When fifteen-year-old Sam winds up on Monad, the first circuit planet of Havona, he must master powerful lessons or he'll be Reset. He's sucked into a black hole and must face off with his Anti-self in order to save himself — and the entire universe! The secrets he learns are essential to surviving this cosmic adventure. In his desperate quest to maintain his identity, he learns more about himself than he ever imagined in this coming-of-age space adventure. Ages 8+

The Wrong Rock: A tale of equality told through the adventure of a mushroom. Martin the Mushroom was born on the wrong rock. He embarks on an epic journey across the sea to get where he feels he belongs, but he doesn't look the same as the local mushrooms, so they push him away. Martin's adventure teaches an inspiring and valuable lesson by exposing the truth that, despite our differences, we are all living on the same rock. 34 pages of full-color images based on artwork from the short animated film of the same name. Ages 2+

Made in United States
North Haven, CT
23 November 2021

11453448R00050